Heart of the Shepherd, Inc.
at Shepherd's Cross

16792 East 450 Road

Claremore, OK 74017-0935

918-342-5911

www.shepherdscross.com

PERCY
The Perfect Pumpkin

Written by Frankie S. Campbell

Illustrated by Bethany Powell

Edited by Dr. Diane Dickinson

Colored by Lea Runnels

Technical Assistance by Whitley Hughes

Provided by Heart of the Shepherd @ Shepherd's Cross

Note from the Author

My name is Frankie S. Campbell. I was born to Frank and Ella Mae Neeley on June 16, 1952. I was raised in the small community of Westville, Oklahoma. My parents were married a number of years before having any children, then had three daughters. Family and children were very special to my parents and I grew up to value that, too.
I married Bob Campbell, my high school sweetheart, in August 1968. Since 1973 we have made our home in and around the Claremore Sequoya area. God blessed us with a daughter and son who have added to our joy by giving us four precious grandchildren.

It was my privilege to stay home with our children while they were growing up. However in 1988 when her daughter began college, I started teaching at a Christian preschool. I immediately fell in love with the children and teaching and have been in Early Childhood Education ever since.
I currently am the Preschool Master Teacher for the Delaware Tribe at Secondine Child Development Center in Chelsea, Oklahoma. My goal is to instill a love for learning and to help each child become strong and confident in problem solving and other life skills.

This is my first book to be published, although I'm also working on a series about the lives of three children during the Oklahoma Land Run. I have also written several short stories and poems. God has blessed me and my family so much. My prayer is for the Lord to use me and my writing to bless others, especially children and their families. I give all praise and glory to the Lord.

About the Illustrator

Bethany Powell is an aspiring novelist. Though not fond of drawing, to make this book a nice souvenir of Shepherd's Cross and fun to read at the Pumpkin Festival, she put in a lot of time first drawing, then inking the pictures you see. She started out without much idea of the factual anatomy of a pumpkin or its vine but began to observe from her family's garden and tried to correct later drafts as she went along!

Bethany worked at Shepherd's Cross, during the time this book was first published. She has since devoted her life to writing full time, and frequently stops in to spin with us for a bit, and share stories of her writing career.

The History of "Percy"

In the fall of 2004 Frankie Campbell brought a group of preschoolers to the Pumpkin Festival at Shepherd's Cross. Her heart was stirred to write this story, for us to share with the children that visit the Pumpkin Patch during the fall celebration at Shepherd's Cross.

The following year when Frankie brought another group of young children to the patch, she also brought the rough draft of "Percy". We are so gratified that she took the time and energy to create this parable for us about celebrating the fall harvest - and the truth of the Lord of the Harvest himself, Jesus Christ.

"A farmer went out to sow his seed."   **Matthew 13:3**

The time every single pumpkin in the patch had been waiting for was almost here! The pumpkin seeds had been planted in the early cool spring, and ever since that day, through the hot summer the pumpkins had grown.

There is a season for every activity under heaven.   *Ecclesiastes 3:1*

Wild storm winds had howled, lightning cracked and thunder crashed. Gentle showers fell to water the seeds. Through this growing season every pumpkin had been looking forward to **harvest time**.

Every pumpkin, that is, except Percy. What did he have to anticipate? Who would ever choose him?

While all the other pumpkins in the patch had grown round and fat and orange, something had gone wrong for Percy.

It couldn't have been the seed itself, because his brothers and sisters on the vine grew plump and round with gorgeous color.

It couldn't be blamed on the soil, because it was loose
and rich and the farmer had cared well for the field.

It wasn't the weather. It seemed that this year the rains fell exactly when needed, and the temperatures had been great. The sun, wind, and rain had all added up to a perfect season for growing pumpkins.

"For I know the plans I have for you," declares the Lord, "plans to prosper you and not to harm you, plans to give you hope and a future."   *Jeremiah 29:11*

So what had been the problem for Percy? He was not perfect. He was not plump and round. He was all crooked and even a little flat on one side! Even his color left something to be desired. And his size was downright puny!

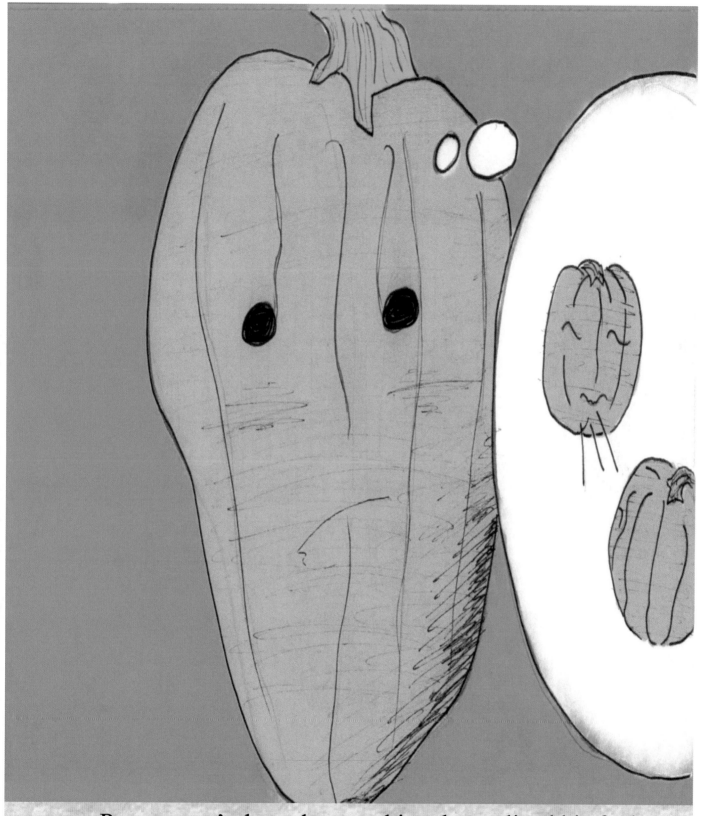

Percy wasn't the only pumpkin who realized his faults. He'd heard the things the other pumpkins had said. Some pumpkins outright laughed and didn't even care that he heard the mean things they said . . . like . . . .

"Who will choose Percy? He is going to lay right here in the patch and rot. No one will choose him. He won't even make a decent pie! Ha-ha-ha !"

"They are like a scarecrow in a melon patch... Do not fear them; they can do no harm..." Jeremiah10:5

Some of the other pumpkins were kinder, but still hurtful - they just whispered things about Percy. Some felt sorry for Percy. Even that hurt. Percy didn't want their pity.

So he was known as Poor, Puny Percy Pumpkin! The pumpkin that no one would want. What did he have to look forward to? Percy spent every day sad and dreading the thought of Harvest.

"Open your eyes and look at the fields. They are ripe for the harvest" John 4:35

But plans were being made and things were happening on the farm. Everyone could feel the excitement in the air. Days were cooler and filled with activity. The vines had served their purpose and began to dry up. Harvest time was here, ready or not.

Percy was *not* ready.

The farmer, his family and some workers all showed up one day to gather up the pumpkins. With one quick slash of a sharp knife, Percy was cut from the vine and tossed into a wagon load of other pumpkins. Then the load was taken to an area of the field that had been cleared, where hay bales had been placed.

There Percy and all the other pumpkins were arranged on those bales and on the ground so people could look them over and make their choices. The farmer came to Percy and set him upon a bale of hay and placed others all around him. Later his wife stopped and dusted some rich soil off Percy.

"There," she said. "Now you look better, little pumpkin." And she left.

Night came with a crisp breeze and people began to arrive at the farm. A big bonfire was lit, hot apple cider and pumpkin bread were served, and pumpkins were being chosen right and left.

Pumpkins all around Percy were chosen and taken away.

"I have chosen you out of the world." John 18:19

Soon he was the only pumpkin left on his bale. The farmer's wife walked by and turned Percy over.

"There, little one," she said, "Now your flat side doesn't show so much."

"And hope does not disappoint us, because God has poured out His love into our hearts by the Holy Spirit whom He has given us." Romans 5:5

Percy knew she was being kind, but he felt so ugly and alone. What would happen to him when everyone was gone and all the other pumpkins had been chosen?

Just then, a little boy ran over and stopped right in front of Percy.

"Hey, Daddy! Look! Over here!"

    A tall man with twinkling eyes walked over to Percy's bale. He bent down and picked Percy up in his strong hands. "Oh, no!" said Percy to himself . "Now he will notice my flat side."

    Percy couldn't believe what he heard next! The man put his arm around his son and said, "My son, you have made the right choice. This is the very pumpkin we came looking for."

"For you created my inmost being; you knit me together in my mother's womb. I praise you because I am fearfully and wonderfully made."   *Psalm139:13*

Percy was carried over to the farmer, near the bonfire, where people were paying for pumpkins. Percy thought to himself, "What if in the light of the fire the father and son notice that my color isn't bright orange, or what if they see my crooked shape? He was afraid they would realize their mistake and put him back.

Again, Percy was surprised by what he heard! The father asked the farmer, "How much for this little pumpkin? It is just what we were looking for, right, son?"

The boy was smiling. "Yes, Daddy!"

"...Whatever you did for the least of these brothers of mine, you did for me."
Matthew 26:40

Then the boy turned and spoke to the farmer, "I've been saving up my allowance and doing extra chores so I could pay the price for the pumpkin myself."

He dug out a few crumpled bills and some coins and gave it all to the farmer for his pumpkin. The father carried Percy to the old pick-up, and the son cradled Percy in his lap all the way home.

When they finally got to their little home a few miles away, Percy was carried inside and set on a table. Now what would happen to Percy? In the bright little kitchen, would all Percy's faults be noticed? Would the father and son be disappointed?

"...Let us purify ourselves from everything that contaminates body and spirit, perfecting holiness out of reverence for God."   *2 Corinthians 7:1*

Before Percy knew what was happening, the father cut around his stem with a sharp knife. The son scraped the stringy pulp and all the seeds out of Percy. Then he washed Percy inside and out until Percy was completely clean.

"Now what, Daddy?" said the son. "Our little pumpkin's nice and clean!"

"And we know that in all things God works for the good of those who love Him, who have been called according to His purpose. "   **Romans 8:28**

     "He sure is, son! But we are not through with him, yet," the father said. He went to work on Percy, turning him on his flat side. "Here is the perfect place for a face." Then with the skill of an artist, the father carved a smiling face that was truly awesome.

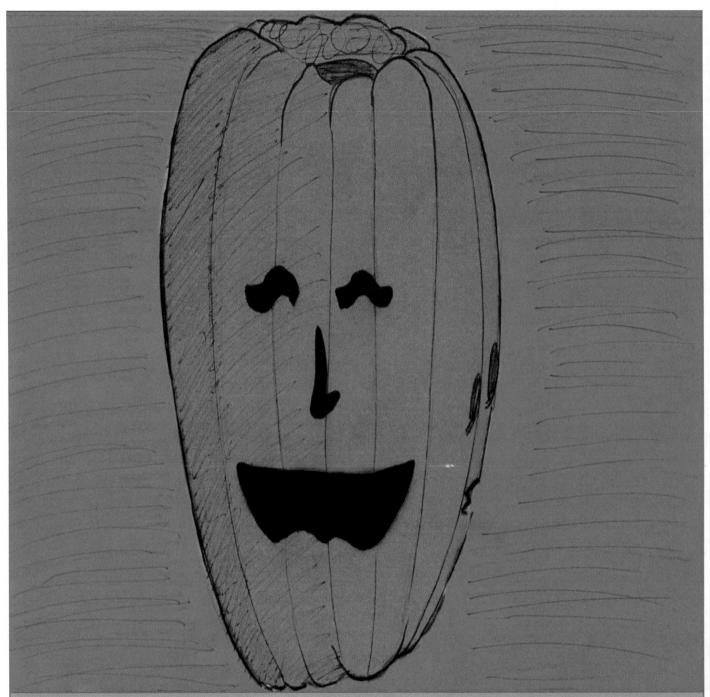

"May the God of hope fill you with all joy and peace as you trust in Him, so that you may overflow with hope by the power of the Holy Spirit."   *Romans 15:13*

"Now are you through, Daddy?" asked the son, "Is our pumpkin finished?"

"Not yet," Smiled his father, "Now our little pumpkin is clean and carved, but look inside. He is empty. No one wants to feel empty. He would feel sad. So, look what I have!"

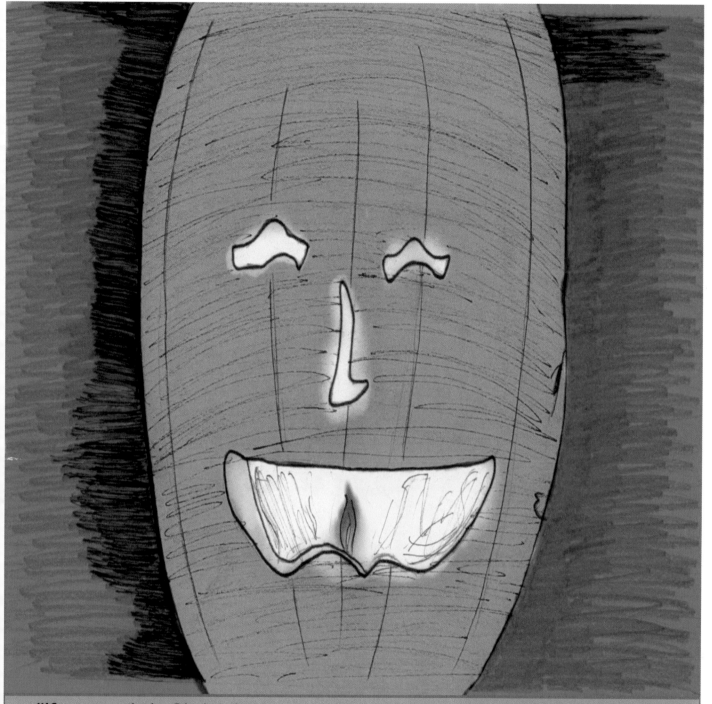

"If anyone is in Christ, he is a new creation; the old has gone, the new has come!"
1 Corinthians 6:17

The father placed a special light inside of Percy and touched the wick with a flame. All of a sudden Percy felt full of warmth! Incredible joy spread through out him! The boy placed the top back on Percy. The light from inside of Percy poured out of his happy face.

"And hope does not disappoint us, because God has poured out his love into our hearts by the
Holy Spirit, whom he has given us."　　　　Romans 5:5

　　"Now," said the father. "Our little pumpkin's light can shine and brighten the way.　All of our friends will see the path and come to our home to enjoy the feast we have made for them. It is good to have a light for our friends,　right, son?"

　　　"Right! We chose well, didn't we, Daddy? He is the perfect little pumpkin," declared the son.

　　　Percy knew he was special after all!

Just as Percy felt less than complete, and not quite good enough, empty - well, sometimes people feel that way, too.

Do you ever feel that way? I have felt that way. Just as Percy was found, brought home, cleaned up, and made to feel special, with his light shining brightly for all the world to see, it can be that way for each of us.

There is a man who came to earth to help make us whole. He felt the pain that we feel. He felt the shame we feel. He wanted to help us, to deliver us from those feelings. This man was more than a man. He gave His life so that we could live free of hopeless feelings, and be filled with love and joy. His name is Jesus.

It is simple to know Him. Just ask Him to come in to your heart and heal your biggest hurts. Then read His words in a book called the Bible, and live like He did, with love, joy and hope in your life. Jesus does not promise that bad things will never happen to us, but He does promise to always be there to comfort us, and help us. He is my very best friend. I hope He is your best friend, too.

If you confess with your mouth "Jesus is Lord," and believe in your heart that God raised Him from the dead,
you will be saved.   Romans 10:9

If you have any questions, let us know.   We would be delighted to visit with you.

Dr. Diane Dickinson, for Heart of the Shepherd Inc.

Made in the USA
Middletown, DE
03 September 2024

60343771R00022